# STONE SOUP

Illustrated by
Diane Paterson

**Troll Associates**

*Library of Congress Cataloging in Publication Data*
Main entry under title:

Stone soup.

    SUMMARY: Arriving in a town where the food has
been hidden, hungry soldiers set about making a
soup of water and stones while the villagers
watch.
    [1. Folklore—France]   I. Paterson, Diane,
1946-
PZ8.1.S863          398.2 '1 '0944          80-27947
ISBN 0-89375-478-1
ISBN 0-89375-479-X (pbk.)

10 9 8 7 6 5 4 3

# STONE SOUP

Long, long ago, in a faraway land, some soldiers were marching home from war. They were very tired, for they had traveled a great distance. They were also very hungry. The soldiers would have welcomed even a small bowl of soup. But how could they make soup? They had nothing to put into a pot except the stones they found in the road. And who ever heard of stone soup?

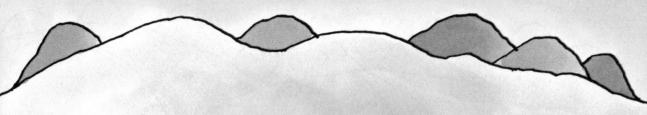

In the distance, the soldiers saw a small village. They thought about the comfortable beds and the delicious foods they might find there, and they walked a little faster.

"I would be happy to get a loaf of warm bread and a nice bed to sleep in," said one soldier.

"I would be glad to get even one slice of bread, and a warm barn to sleep in," said another.

"We will be lucky to find a few stale crusts before we are chased from the village," said the third. He knew that the townspeople would not want to share what they had with strangers.

"Still, we can ask," said the first soldier.

"Yes," agreed the second. "If we do not ask, we will never know."

"All right," said the third. "You will ask. Then you will know."

The townspeople had seen the soldiers coming, and now they were busy hiding their food. They hid their potatoes down in their cellars. They tucked their vegetables under their beds. They stuffed their barley into their pillowcases. They hung their meat inside their closets. And they lowered pails of milk down into the wells. At last, all the food in the entire village was hidden. The villagers went inside their houses and waited.

When the soldiers arrived, they knocked on the first door they saw. "Could you spare some food and a place to sleep?" they asked. But the villagers said they had no extra beds and too little food for themselves. So the soldiers went to the next house, and the next, and the next. The answer was always the same. There was no food. There was no place to sleep.

Then one of the soldiers had an idea. "Good villagers," he called, "since you have no food, perhaps you will let us borrow a large cooking pot. Then we can make a pot of stone soup."

"Stone soup?" whispered the villagers. "Who ever heard of stone soup?"

"This is something we must find out about," whispered the mayor. "Someone bring a pot. Quickly!"

When the pot had been brought to the village square, the soldiers filled it with water, and built a fire beneath it. "Finding good soup stones is the most important part," they said. Then they looked, and they looked. Finally, each soldier found some nice smooth stones. They put the stones into the pot and brought the water to a boil. Then they sniffed.

"Something is missing," said the first soldier.

"Yes," agreed the second. "But what?"

"Salt and pepper," said the third, sniffing the soup. Then he turned to the villagers and said, "We know you have no food, but could you find a bit of pepper and some salt? Pepper and salt will bring out the flavor of the soup stones."

At once, the mayor's wife disappeared and came back with some salt and pepper.

"Thank you," said the soldiers, as they shook the salt and pepper into the pot. "It smells better already."

They all sniffed the soup. Then one of the soldiers said, "A good stone soup should have some onions. But since there are none, we will simply do without them."

A peasant woman heard the soldier and said, "I may have an onion or two," and she hurried home. Soon, she returned with half a dozen peeled onions, which she dropped into the soup.

"This will be a good stone soup," said the soldiers. "It's a pity we don't have any celery. But that would be hoping for too much. After all, we were lucky to find such good soup stones in the first place."

A farmer's wife heard this and ran home. In a few minutes, she returned with several stalks of celery, which she cut into small pieces and tossed into the soup.

After a while, the first soldier said, "Something is lacking."

"There are no carrots," agreed the second.

"But there is no sense in asking for something that no one has," added the third.

Then a peasant said, "Carrots? I might just have one or two carrots at home." And he ran off to get them. He returned with several crisp orange carrots, which he sliced into the soup.

"The stones are cooking nicely," remarked the soldiers. "Just smell the soup! Too bad we don't have a few potatoes. But why wish for something you can't get?"

A farmer overheard this and hurried away. Soon he was back, with an armful of potatoes. The soldiers peeled them and tossed them into the soup.

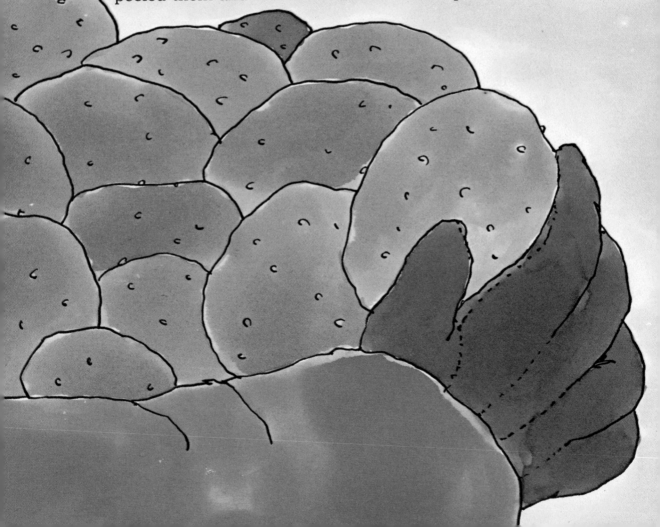

Then the first soldier stirred the soup, saying, "It is a bit too thin, but since there is no barley to thicken it, we will have to be satisfied." The town miller heard this and ran to his mill. Soon he returned with some barley, which he stirred into the soup.

"A perfect stone soup," said the first soldier.

"If only it were a bit richer," suggested the second soldier. "Too bad we have no milk to stir in." And before long, someone had brought him a bucket of milk for the soup.

The third soldier said, "With a bit of meat, it would be just like the soup we made for the king last month! But since there is no meat, we must be content with what we have."

The villagers buzzed with excitement. The soldiers had dined with the king! The townspeople ran to their houses and came back with big chunks of meat, which they put into the soup.

When at last the stone soup was ready, the soldiers tasted it.

"It is thick," said the first.

"It is rich," said the second.

"It is fit for a king," said the third.

Now the villagers decided that if the soup were really fit for a king, then it could not be served alone. So they brought out loaves of bread and roasts and barrels of cider. Long tables were set in the village square, and everyone sat down to eat. And all the villagers agreed that the soup was thick, rich, and fit for a king. They could hardly believe it had been made from stones!

They ate and drank and danced well into the night. Then they took the soldiers into their homes and let them sleep in the most comfortable beds. In the morning, everyone gathered again in the village square.

"Thank you for everything," said the soldiers.

"We want to thank *you*," said the mayor. "You have taught us something important."

"Goodbye," called the soldiers, as they headed down the road.

"Goodbye," called the mayor.

"Imagine," whispered the townspeople. "Thick, rich soup—made from stones! No one will ever believe it. After all, who ever heard of stone soup?"